For CHJ and JHS

Other titles by Clare Jarrett:
Catherine and the Lion
Dancing Maddy

First published in hardback in Great Britain by HarperCollins Publishers Ltd in 2001
First published in paperback in Great Britain by Collins Picture Books Ltd in 2002
Collins Picture Books is an imprint of the Children's Division, part of HarperCollins Publishers Ltd.

1 3 5 7 9 10 8 6 4 2
ISBN: 0 00 664768 5

The HarperCollins website address is: www.fireandwater.com

Printed and bound in Singapore

JAMIE
and the lost bird

Clare Jarrett

Collins

An imprint of HarperCollins*Publishers*

One stormy evening a strange bird walked in through the gate and up the path.

"What's that tapping sound?" asked Jamie.

Grandfather opened the door.

"My goodness me!" he said to the bird. "You must be freezing with no feathers or coat. Come in."

Jamie fetched some towels. "We must get him warm and dry," he said.

"He looks hungry," said Jamie.

"Do you think he'll eat spaghetti?" asked Grandfather.

"Worms would be better," said Jamie. He put his coat on and went out to find some.

The bird was very hungry.

"He needs a name," said Grandfather.

Jamie looked around at his toys. "How about Thomas?" he said.

"My father's name was Thomas," said Grandfather. "What do you think, Thomas?"

The bird looked up. "Chirp," he said.

"Where will Thomas sleep?" Jamie asked.

Grandfather rummaged about in a cupboard.

"Here we are!" he said at last. "Not too big and not too small."

"And he can have my old jumper," said Jamie, tucking it into the box.

Thomas settled himself in and was soon fast asleep.

In the morning they took Thomas to the vet.

"He needs to be checked over, and we need some advice," said Grandfather. "I've never looked after a bird before."

"Mmm," said the vet. "He'll be fine. Plenty of good food, fresh air and exercise."

They bought a large bag of food, a special bowl and some seeds.

"Seeds will make his feathers grow glossy and strong," said Grandfather.

"So he *will* grow some?" asked Jamie.

"Oh yes," said Grandfather, "given time."

Thomas soon felt at home. He liked to help around the house. But sometimes he got in the way.

One evening
during supper
Thomas landed
in the butter,
by accident.

"Oh dear," said
Grandfather, in dismay.
"I think he needs his
own house," said Jamie.
"Chirp," said Thomas.

Later that night, Thomas sat on Grandfather's head. Grandfather woke up with a start.

"Thomas," he said, "this is *too* much."

He got up, went downstairs, and started to draw a plan for Thomas' house.

The next day
Grandfather and
Jamie collected bits
of wood, nails,
tiles and paint.
Thomas helped as
much as he could.

He found a chimney pot.
"I don't think you'll
need that," said Jamie.

"But these will be very useful," said
Grandfather, pulling out a set of wheels.

At last the house was finished. Jamie stood by,
while Grandfather got his camera ready for the
grand opening. Off came the sheet.

Flash! went the camera.

Thomas walked up and down the ramp, crowing and chortling.

"He likes it!" shouted Jamie.

"Quite right," said Grandfather, "I wouldn't mind living there myself."

The next time Jamie came to stay with
Grandfather, Thomas had changed.

"Oh, Thomas, what beautiful feathers,"
said Jamie.

Thomas puffed himself up so that his
feathers glistened and shone in the sunlight.

"Chirp, chirp, chirrup," said Thomas.

"Oh, yes,"
said Jamie,
"and I've
missed you
too."

"It's time for a photograph," said Grandfather.

Suddenly there was a terrible commotion. "Chirp, *pock-pock-pock*, chirp, chirrup, *pock*."

"Go and see what's bothering Thomas, Jamie," said Grandfather.

Jamie peered into the little house. "Thomas!" he cried. "I didn't think you could do that."

"Well I never," said Grandfather. "He's laid you a beautiful, brown egg."

"Grandfather," said Jamie seriously, "Thomas is a girl."

"We'll just have to call him Thomasina then," said Grandfather.

"*Pock-pock-pock*, chirrup, *pock*," said Thomas.

Little Pig Figwort

HENRIETTA BRANFORD

ILLUSTRATED BY
CLAUDIO MUÑOZ

WHOSE House?

A lift-the-flap book

Colin and Jacqui Hawkins

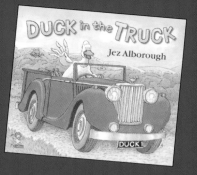

DUCK in the TRUCK

Jez Alborough

DUCK 1

WHERE'S TIM'S TED?

Ian Whybrow
Illustrated by Russell Ayto

Every child deserves the best...

Mucky Pup

KEN BROWN

I Love You, Blue Kangaroo!

EMMA CHICHESTER CLARK

shortlisted for the prestigious Kate Greenaway Medal.

Collins

Picture books

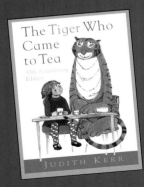

The Tiger Who Came to Tea

40th Anniversary Edition

JUDITH KERR

THE SECOND PRINCESS

2

Hiawyn Oram and Tony Ross

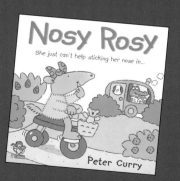

Nosy Rosy

She just can't help sticking her nose in...

Peter Curry

snore!

Michael Rosen & Jonathan Langley